Kids Can Cook

MID-ATLANTIC
RECIPES

Joanne Mattern

Mitchell Lane
PUBLISHERS

Mid-Atlantic • Midwestern
New England • Pacific Northwest
Southwestern • Western
Recipes

Copyright © 2012 by Mitchell Lane Publishers

PUBLISHER'S NOTE: The facts on which this book is based have been thoroughly researched. Documentation of such research can be found on page 60. While every possible effort has been made to ensure accuracy, the publisher will not assume liability for damages caused by inaccuracies in the data, and makes no warranty on the accuracy of the information contained herein.

Library of Congress
Mattern, Joanne, 1963–
 Mid-Atlantic recipes / by Joanne Mattern.
     p. cm. — (Kids can cook)
 Includes bibliographical references and index.
 ISBN 978-1-61228-068-4 (library bound)
 1. Cooking, American—Juvenile literature.
 2. Cooking—Middle Atlantic States—Juvenile literature. I. Title.
 TX715.M11594 2012
 641.5974—dc23

                                        2011034432

eBook ISBN: 9781612281629

Printing   1   2   3   4   5   6   7   8   9

                                        PLB

THE MENU

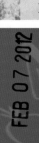

Journey to the Mid-Atlantic States and you'll discover a range of landforms. Most of the Mid-Atlantic States border the Atlantic Ocean, so parts of the area feature coastlines and beaches. Even people who don't live near the ocean have access to water, though, thanks to the Chesapeake Bay and Delaware Bay in the southern part of the region; the Hudson River in New York and New Jersey; the Susquehanna River in Maryland and Pennsylvania; the Potomac River in Virginia and Washington, D.C.; and the Great Lakes in northern New York. Travel inland from the coast and you'll find mountains, forests, and marshes. These habitats are home to a huge variety of plants and animals, many of which have shaped the foods of this region.

Native Americans were the first settlers in the Mid-Atlantic and the first to cultivate the bounty of food. Algonquin tribes planted corn, beans, tobacco, and squash. They also fished, trapped oysters and crabs, and hunted deer and other animals, both large and small. Native American groups such as the Lenni-Lenape farmed pumpkins and other types of squash, watermelons, sweet potatoes, and beans. They also grew sunflowers and used the seeds for bread. Corn was an especially useful food that could also be made into cake or bread.

As Dutch, English, and French settlers came to the region beginning in the 1500s, they discovered a land of new foods. Helpful Native

Americans taught their ways to these immigrants, and soon the settlers were growing and enjoying foods they had never tasted before, such as corn and tomatoes. The settlers cultivated fruits such as apples, strawberries, cherries, plums, and peaches. They used them to make jams and jellies and also baked them into pies and muffins.

Europeans shared their food traditions too. They brought vegetables such as carrots, cabbages, and turnips to the New World. As the centuries passed, more immigrants came, from countries such as Ireland, Sweden, The Netherlands, and Germany. Later they were joined by Italian, Irish, and Polish immigrants, and by people from Asia. All added their own ethnic twist to foods. Sausages (German), pasta (Italian), dumplings (Asian), and rye bread and bagels (Jewish) are just a few examples of ethnic cooking that became popular in the Mid-Atlantic region. Today, ethnic communities thrive in big cities and small towns, and European favorites, such as the German pretzel and the Italian spaghetti-and-meatball dinner, are popular not just in this region but all across the United States.

African Americans brought their own food traditions from Africa and the Caribbean, and developed them in the South. During the difficult days of slavery, people learned to use what was at hand, and they added spices and fat to improve the flavor and nutrition of poor-quality foods. After slavery was abolished and the Civil War was over, many African Americans moved north, adding their Southern-style recipes to the Mid-Atlantic's food traditions.

Ever since the first settlers arrived, the Mid-Atlantic region has been a rich farming country. At one time nine out of ten residents lived on farms. Farms had storehouses to keep smoked foods. Farmers preserved vegetables and fruits to be used well past harvest time. They also learned to rely on foods such as apples and squash, which were harvested in late summer and early fall and would last through the long winter when other fresh foods were not available.

The Mid-Atlantic region has been called "the crossroads of American cooking." Each state in this region has its own special foods and traditions. New Jersey may be the most crowded state in terms of people per square mile, but most of the state is actually farmland. It is called the Garden State because it is a leading producer of spinach, peaches, apples, asparagus, squash, cranberries, and tomatoes. These flavorful fruits and vegetables have found their way into many tasty salads, desserts, and other dishes.

New York is one of the largest producers of apples in the nation, and it also has many dairy farms. Two of America's favorite snacks, potato chips and Buffalo wings, were invented in New York State. New York City, with its waves of immigrants arriving in New York Harbor, is home to delicatessens featuring corned beef and pastrami, and with its Fulton Fish Market, fresh seafood is readily available.

Facing religious persecution and invited by William Penn, immigrants from Germany settled in Pennsylvania hundreds of years ago. These religious communities, including the Amish and the Mennonites, made a specialty of serving hearty food. The motto of the Amish is "Fill yourself up, clean your plate," and this group is famous for "having a fancy way with ordinary things." German dishes such as sauerkraut (pickled cabbage), waffles, and apple butter (a jam made from apples and cinnamon) are just a few of the foods introduced by the Amish. They are also famous for pancakes loaded with fruits and nuts.

Just south of Pennsylvania is Delaware, one of the largest chicken producers in the nation. The Chesapeake Bay area of Maryland also has rich food traditions, including crab feasts and clambakes that feature the clams, oysters, and rockfish (striped bass) found in the waters nearby. Virginia, another farming state, is famous for its ham and peanuts.

Washington, D.C., is also part of the Mid-Atlantic region. The nation's capital has been home to more than 40 presidents, who brought their own traditions and food favorites to the White House.

This book takes you on a journey through some of the most popular and interesting foods in the Mid-Atlantic area. Enjoy cooking and eating these dishes and sharing a tasty part of American history!

Before You Start

Many of the recipes in this book involve the use of sharp knives, hot ovens, and boiling water or hot oil. Be sure to work with **an adult** as you prepare these recipes. Frying is especially dangerous because hot oil can spatter out of the pan, so it is always important to have an adult nearby for safety. Wear protective clothing such as long sleeves and oven mitts, and always keep pot handles over the counter, not hanging over the edge.

It is also important to read the entire recipe before you start. Have all your foods laid out and ready at the start of the recipe. You should also take out whatever bowls, pans, utensils, and other equipment you need before you start cooking. Being prepared will help make your cooking journey easier and more fun.

Please work with an adult whenever a recipe calls for using a knife, a stove or oven, or boiling water.

Potato Chips

In August 1853, George Crum was a chef at Moon Lake Lodge in Saratoga Springs, New York. When a customer complained that Crum had sliced his French fries too thick, Crum got angry. He sliced a potato as thin as he could and fried it until it was crispy. Customers loved this new treat, and the potato chip was born!

Preparation Time: 8 minutes
Cooking Time: 15 minutes
Makes: Approximately
64 potato chips

Ingredients

2 baking potatoes, washed (and peeled, if desired)
Bowl of ice water
32 ounces cooking oil
Salt

1. Slice the potatoes into thin rounds (about $1/8$ inch thick). Place them in a bowl of ice water to keep them from sticking together and turning brown.
2. Heat oil in a deep pan or electric deep fryer set to 375°F.
3. Pat potato slices completely dry on a paper towel so that they do not make the hot oil spatter.
4. Fry a few slices at a time until they are crisp and golden brown.
5. Scoop out the chips with a slotted spoon and drain them on paper towels.
6. Add salt to taste and serve.

Soft Pretzels

Pretzels were invented in southern France or northern Italy by a Franciscan monk. During Lent, it was forbidden to cook with fat, eggs, or milk. The monk decided to make a dough out of only flour, salt, and water. Then he twisted the dough into the shape of two arms crossed in prayer. He named the treat *pretiola,* which is Latin for "little gift." The first pretzels were given out to children as a reward for saying their prayers. Rumor has it that pretzels may have been brought to North America by the Puritans on the *Mayflower,* although other sources say pretzels were first made in America by a German baker named Jochem Wessel in 1652. Early settlers often sold pretzels to Native Americans, who really loved this new treat. Soft pretzels are very popular today and can often be bought from street vendors in large cities.

Preparation Time: 15 minutes
Cooking Time: 15 minutes
Makes: 12 pretzels

Ingredients

1 package active dry yeast
1½ cups warm water
1 tablespoon sugar
4 cups flour
1 tablespoon salt
1 egg
Kosher salt

1. Sprinkle yeast over water in a small bowl.
2. Stir in sugar.
3. While the yeast begins to bubble, slowly mix in flour and salt to make a stiff dough.
4. Turn mixture out onto a counter or large cutting board and knead until smooth.
5. Pinch dough into 12 balls. Roll each ball into a long rope and twist into a pretzel shape.
6. Place on a lightly greased cookie sheet.
7. Beat an egg in a bowl and brush egg onto each pretzel.
8. Bake 15 minutes at 400°F or until brown.
9. While pretzels are still warm, press Kosher salt over the surface.
10. Cool and enjoy!

Buffalo Wings

Buffalo wings are popular all across the country, but they got their start in 1964 in Buffalo, New York. There are several stories about how this recipe was invented, but most of them revolve around the Bellissimo family, owners of the Anchor Bar and Restaurant in Buffalo. With an abundance of wings prepared for the soup pot, Teressa Bellissimo decided to try something new—and Buffalo wings were born.

Instead of frying, you can bake these wings at 400°F for 35 minutes or until juices run clear.

Preparation Time: 15 minutes
Cooking Time: 30 to 45 minutes
Serves: 6

Ingredients

> 4 pounds chicken wings, tips discarded
> Freshly ground black pepper
> Salt (if desired)
> 4 cups vegetable oil
> Unsalted butter
> Red pepper sauce
> Celery sticks
> Blue cheese dressing (or substitute ranch dressing)

1. Wash the chicken wings. Chop each one in half, cutting through the joint.
2. Dry the wings with paper towels, then sprinkle them with freshly ground black pepper and, if desired, salt.

For mild wings, melt 3 parts butter and add 1 part red pepper sauce.
For medium wings, use equal amounts of butter and red pepper sauce.
For hot wings, melt 1 part butter and add 3 parts red pepper sauce.
For Buffalo style (very hot!), skip the butter and just use the red pepper sauce.

3. Heat the oil in a deep pan or deep fryer until it starts to pop and sizzle (around 400°F). Add half the chicken wings and cook until they are golden and crisp, stirring or shaking them every once in a while.
4. When the wings are done, remove them and let them drain on paper towels.
5. Cook the rest of the wings in the same way.
6. Melt butter in a heavy saucepan over medium heat. Add the hot sauce according to taste (see the tip box, above). Stir and remove from heat.
7. Place the chicken in a plastic bowl with a sealable lid. Pour the sauce on top. Close the lid and hold it tight, then shake it until chicken is evenly coated.
8. Serve with celery sticks and dressing—and lots of napkins!

Virginia
Peanut Brittle

Peanuts originated in Peru or Brazil more than 3,500 years ago. Spanish and Portuguese explorers brought them to North America, Europe, and Africa. Southern U.S. farmers originally grew peanuts as feed for livestock, but when Civil War soldiers used them for food, this nut became popular throughout the Mid-Atlantic region. In the early 1900s, new machines were being used to harvest and clean the peanuts, and demand increased to include oil, roasted and salted nuts, peanut butter, and candy. Virginia produced its first commercial crop of peanuts in the 1840s, and today there are more than 3,000 peanut farms in the state.

This recipe calls for roasted peanuts. If you use raw peanuts, add them with the corn syrup and water in step 3.

Preparation Time: 15 minutes
Cooking Time: 10 minutes
Serves: 8

Ingredients

2 cups roasted, unsalted,
    shelled peanuts
2 cups sugar
1 cup light corn syrup
1 cup water
$\frac{1}{8}$ teaspoon salt
1 tablespoon butter
1 teaspoon vanilla extract
1 tablespoon baking soda

1. Butter the bottom and sides of a jelly roll pan and set it aside.
2. Spread the peanuts on a cutting board and crush them with a rolling pin.
3. Put the sugar into a skillet. Stir in corn syrup and water.

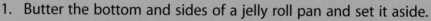

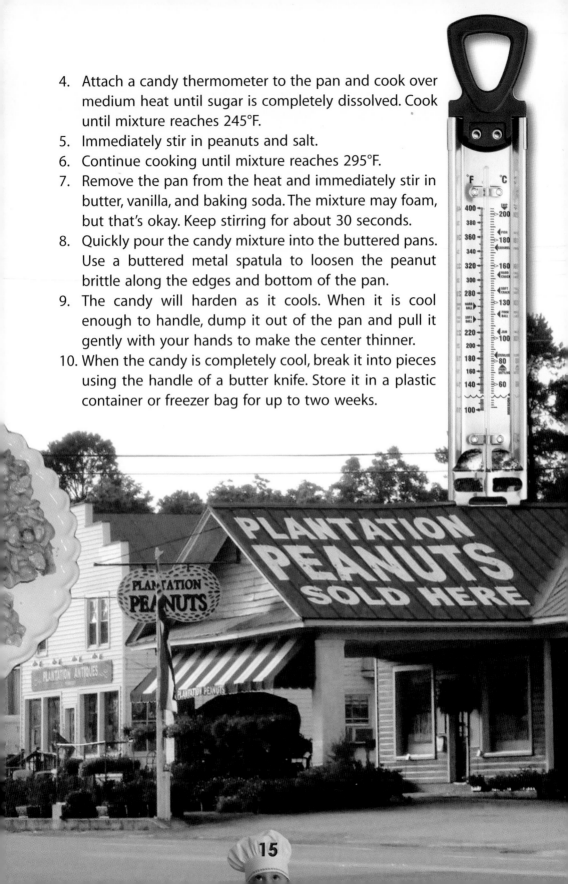

4. Attach a candy thermometer to the pan and cook over medium heat until sugar is completely dissolved. Cook until mixture reaches 245°F.
5. Immediately stir in peanuts and salt.
6. Continue cooking until mixture reaches 295°F.
7. Remove the pan from the heat and immediately stir in butter, vanilla, and baking soda. The mixture may foam, but that's okay. Keep stirring for about 30 seconds.
8. Quickly pour the candy mixture into the buttered pans. Use a buttered metal spatula to loosen the peanut brittle along the edges and bottom of the pan.
9. The candy will harden as it cools. When it is cool enough to handle, dump it out of the pan and pull it gently with your hands to make the center thinner.
10. When the candy is completely cool, break it into pieces using the handle of a butter knife. Store it in a plastic container or freezer bag for up to two weeks.

Waldorf Salad

This simple and refreshing salad gets its name from New York City's famous Waldorf Hotel (it is now called the Waldorf-Astoria). Most food historians believe that Oscar Tschirky, who was in charge of the hotel's dining room, created the salad around 1893.

If you add a cup of diced cooked chicken to this recipe, you can turn this salad into a main course.

Preparation Time: 15 minutes
Serves: 6

Ingredients

½ cup mayonnaise (or
   substitute plain yogurt)
1 teaspoon lemon juice
Pepper to taste
2 cups cored and diced
   apples
1 cup chopped celery
1 cup raisins or red grapes
½ cup walnuts, broken
   into pieces
Fresh lettuce, washed

1. Stir together mayonnaise, lemon juice, and pepper.
2. Combine apples, celery, raisins, and mayonnaise mixture in a large bowl. Stir, then chill until ready to serve.
3. Remove from refrigerator, stir in walnuts, and serve on beds of lettuce.

Fruit Salad

This salad is easy to make and features many of the fruits grown in New Jersey, the Garden State. It's a great snack or dessert on a hot summer day!

Preparation Time: 15 minutes
Serves: 6 to 8

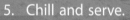

Ingredients

8 ounces strawberries
1 bunch seedless grapes
8 ounces blueberries
½ small watermelon
½ honeydew melon
½ cantaloupe
Lemon juice

1. Wash strawberries, grapes, and blueberries.
2. Slice the strawberries and grapes.
3. Cut each melon into balls using a melon scoop, or dice them.
4. Mix the fruit in a large serving bowl. Sprinkle with lemon juice.
5. Chill and serve.

German Hot Potato Salad

While some potato salads are served cold, the German version is served hot and includes bacon and hard-boiled eggs. This dish is a favorite of Amish cooks in the Lancaster area of Pennsylvania, and its fame has spread throughout the Mid-Atlantic region.

Preparation Time: 10 minutes
Cooking Time: 25 minutes
Serves: 6

Ingredients

3 eggs
6 medium potatoes
8 slices bacon
1 large onion, chopped
3 tablespoons flour
½ cup vinegar
1 cup water
1 tablespoon sugar
½ teaspoon salt
½ teaspoon black pepper

1. Place eggs and water in a saucepan. Bring water to a boil and boil for 5 minutes. Drain and cover with cold water, set aside.
2. Peel the potatoes and boil them in a second saucepan until just tender. Drain and allow to cool. Then cut potatoes into ¼-inch-thick slices.
3. Fry bacon in the skillet until crisp. Remove and drain on paper towels. Save 3 tablespoons of the bacon drippings.
4. Cook the onion in the bacon drippings until tender.
5. Add flour and cook, stirring constantly until flour begins to brown.

6. Stir in vinegar, water, sugar, salt, and pepper. Bring mixture to a boil, then simmer until it begins to thicken.
7. Peel and slice the hard-boiled eggs.
8. Place the potatoes, eggs, and bacon in a serving bowl and mix.
9. Pour the hot dressing over the potato mixture. Stir and serve.

Chicken and Slippery Dumplings

This recipe is popular in Delaware, which is a major supplier of young chickens, called broilers or fryers. The original recipe calls for making dumplings out of vegetable shortening, salt, flour, and hot water, but we've substituted Bisquick® baking mix to make things easier. You could also use the dough from the Beaten Biscuits recipe on page 46.

Preparation Time: 20 minutes
Cooking Time: 1 hour
Serves: 6

Ingredients

- 2 broiler-fryer chickens, cut up, or 4–5 pounds chicken legs and thighs, cut up
- 4 celery stalks, chopped
- 1 medium onion, chopped
- 4 carrots, chopped
- 1 tablespoon chicken bouillon granules
- 2 teaspoons poultry seasoning
- 2 cups Bisquick® baking mix
- ⅔ cup milk

1. Season chicken with salt and pepper, then place chicken and the next five ingredients into a large pot. Cover them with water. Bring the pot to a boil, then turn it down to simmer.
2. When chicken is almost done (after about 45 minutes), stir together the baking mix and milk to make a soft dough.
3. Drop spoonfuls of dough into the boiling broth. Reduce heat to medium.
4. Cook for 10 to 15 minutes, until dumplings are soft and fluffy and the chicken is cooked through.

Philly Cheesesteak

Philadelphia is famous for its cheesesteak sandwich, which you can buy from street vendors and find in many restaurants throughout the city. Pat Olivieri made the first Philly cheesesteak in 1930. He sold sandwiches and hot dogs in an Italian neighborhood in South Philly, and his restaurant is still there, open 24 hours a day. It is run by one of his grandsons.

Although you can buy processed steak sandwich meat in the frozen foods department, fresh-sliced rib-eye from the butcher will give you the authentic Philly flavor. Traditional cheesesteaks are made with Cheez Whiz® processed cheese spread, but many Philadelphians will opt for American or Provolone cheese instead.

Preparation Time: 5 minutes
Cooking Time: 6 minutes per sandwich
Serves: 4

Ingredients

- 1 pound rib-eye steak, sliced paper thin (if you don't see it sliced like this in the store, you can ask your butcher to slice it for you; you can also partially freeze the steak to make it easier to slice thin yourself, with the help of **an adult**)
- 1 tablespoon butter or vegetable oil
- 1 large onion, sliced thin
- Black pepper
- Salt or Worcestershire sauce (this sauce is salty, so use either the salt or the sauce, not both)
- 4 Italian rolls, about 6 inches long
- 4–6 slices American or Provolone cheese, or one can Cheez Whiz® processed cheese spread
- Ketchup, mayonnaise, shredded lettuce, and sliced tomato (optional)

1. Melt the butter or oil in a skillet and add one quarter of the meat. Season with pepper and salt or Worcestershire sauce.
2. Cook for about one minute, constantly turning the meat with a spatula. Add a handful of onion slices and continue cooking and turning until the onions are tender (about 3 minutes).
3. Push the meat and onions together so that they are about the same length and width as the bun. Top with a layer of cheese. Cover the pan for about 30 seconds or until cheese is melted.
4. Cut open the rolls about three-quarters of the way through. Add ketchup, mayonnaise, or any other sauce you wish.
5. Gently transfer the cheesesteak filling to the roll.
6. Top with lettuce and tomato, if desired.

Manhattan Clam Chowder

Chowders are popular soups all over the country, but each area makes its own version. While New England and other shore areas insist that fish chowders be made with a milk-based broth, the island of Manhattan (part of New York City) is famous for a chowder using tomatoes. Food historians believe that Manhattan clam chowder first became popular when it was served at a famous city restaurant called Delmonico's. In 1889, Delmonico's chef Alessandro Filippini published a cookbook that included a recipe for a tomato-based chowder, and the style of soup became well known after that. During the 1890s, Manhattan clam chowder was sometimes called Coney Island Clam Chowder or Fulton Market Clam Chowder, but it later became known by the name we still use today.

Preparation Time: 15 minutes
Cooking Time: 40 minutes
Serves: 6

Ingredients

2 6.5-ounce cans minced clams
1½ cups water
1 16-ounce can diced tomatoes
1 cup onion, chopped fine
⅓ cup celery, chopped fine
2 potatoes, peeled and diced
½ cup carrots, chopped fine
3 tablespoons fresh parsley, chopped
1 teaspoon dried thyme
Dash Worchestershire sauce
1 teaspoon salt
Ground black pepper to taste

1. Drain clams and save liquid. Add water to liquid to make 3 cups of broth.

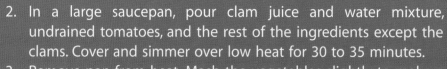

2. In a large saucepan, pour clam juice and water mixture, undrained tomatoes, and the rest of the ingredients except the clams. Cover and simmer over low heat for 30 to 35 minutes.

3. Remove pan from heat. Mash the vegetables slightly to make a thicker broth.

4. Add clams and gently reheat soup (do not let it boil), stirring occasionally.

5. Pour into bowls and serve hot.

Crab Cakes

In the early spring, blue crabs begin to migrate from the Atlantic Ocean into the Chesapeake Bay to molt, mate, and lay their eggs. By the end of the summer, the crabs are large and heavy, and historically they were plentiful. While the Chesapeake Bay is the most well known area for harvesting blue crabs, these colorful crustaceans range along the Atlantic coast from Nova Scotia to Argentina. In the Mid-Atlantic region, steamed crabs served with hot buttered corn on the cob are popular at summer parties. Crab cakes, which are easier to eat, are often featured at festivals and other celebrations.

Instead of frying, you can cook these crab cakes under a broiler. Either way, they taste great with a garden salad, or on a bun with lettuce, tomato, and tartar sauce.

Preparation Time: 10 minutes
Cooking Time: 10 minutes
Serves: 4 to 6

Ingredients

- 1 pound lump crabmeat
- 1 egg
- 2 tablespoons mayonnaise
- ½ teaspoon yellow mustard
- 2 teaspoons Old Bay® Seasoning
  (or substitute Phillips® Seafood Seasoning)
- 2 teaspoons parsley flakes
- 2 slices white bread, crumbled (some people remove the crusts first)
- 3 tablespoons cooking oil

1. Carefully sift through the crabmeat to remove any cartilage or missed shell pieces.
2. Whisk the egg with the mayonnaise, mustard, Old Bay® Seasoning, and parsley.

3. Stir in the crumbled bread.
4. Gently fold in the crabmeat. Try not to break the meat apart as you combine.
5. Use your hands to shape 4 to 6 crab patties.
6. Heat cooking oil in a skillet until hot. Drop in crab cakes. When one side is golden brown, use a spatula to flip the cakes over to cook the other side.
7. Remove and place on a serving dish.

Spaghetti and Meatballs
with Garlic Bread

Many Italian immigrants settled in the New York and New Jersey areas in the late 1800s and early 1900s. Of course, they brought their food traditions with them. Pasta, including spaghetti, is a staple food in many Italian meals. While many cooks make their pasta and sauce (or, as many Italians say, "macaroni and gravy") from scratch, this recipe uses prepared products to make it easier to cook a delicious and popular Italian meal.

Preparation Time: 20 minutes
Cooking Time: 30 to 40 minutes
Serves: 6 to 8

Ingredients

Meatballs:
1½ pounds ground beef
   or meatloaf mix
1 cup breadcrumbs
1 medium onion, chopped fine
⅓ cup chopped fresh parsley
¼ cup water
1 egg
1 tablespoon Worcestershire sauce
½ teaspoon garlic powder
1 teaspoon salt
½ teaspoon pepper
1 tablespoon cooking oil

Pasta:
1 pound spaghetti
½ teaspoon salt
4 cups jarred spaghetti sauce
Italian seasoning

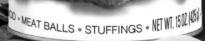

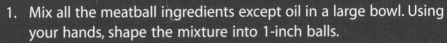

1. Mix all the meatball ingredients except oil in a large bowl. Using your hands, shape the mixture into 1-inch balls.
2. Heat oil in a frying pan.
3. When oil is hot, drop in meatballs. Roll them to brown all around.

4. Pour spaghetti sauce over the meatballs and add Italian seasoning to taste. Cover the pan and continue cooking for about 20 minutes.
5. Meanwhile, cook spaghetti according to package directions. While it's cooking, start the garlic bread.
6. Drain the pasta and serve, topped with meatballs and sauce.

Garlic Bread:

1 loaf Italian bread
½ stick of butter
2 tablespoons garlic powder (or 2 cloves of fresh, chopped fine)
2 tablespoons grated Parmesan cheese

Garlic Bread:

1. Preheat oven to 350°F.
2. Cut Italian bread in half lengthwise.
3. Slice butter thin and spread it over the bread. Sprinkle with garlic and Parmesan cheese.
4. Close the bread halves together, butter sides in. Wrap the loaf in aluminum foil.
5. Bake for 20 minutes.
6. Unwrap the bread and slice it. Arrange it on a plate and serve.

Spiedies

Although spiedies (pronounced "speedies") are not well known outside of central New York, this dish is so popular in the Binghamton, New York, area that there is a three-day festival dedicated to it. Spiedies are similar to shish kebabs in the way they are cooked, but they are usually eaten as a sandwich. The roll is used to hold the meat while the diner pulls out the skewer.

If you don't have access to an outdoor grill, you can cook these under the broiler. Just be sure to keep turning them as you would on a grill.

Preparation Time: 15 minutes
Marinate: At least 2 hours or overnight
Cooking Time: 20 minutes
Serves: 4

Ingredients

1 pound pork, beef, lamb, venison,
    or turkey, cut into 1-inch cubes
$\frac{1}{4}$ cup lemon juice
$\frac{1}{3}$ cup olive oil
$\frac{1}{4}$ cup vinegar
2 cloves garlic, chopped
1 tablespoon basil
1 tablespoon parsley
$\frac{1}{2}$ teaspoon oregano
$\frac{1}{2}$ teaspoon garlic salt
$\frac{1}{2}$ teaspoon salt
$\frac{1}{2}$ teaspoon pepper
4 soft Italian rolls or hot dog rolls

1. Place meat in a large, resealable plastic bag or container. Add all other ingredients except rolls. Seal and shake until well combined. Place the bag or container in the refrigerator to marinate for several hours or overnight.
2. If using wooden skewers, soak them in water for 10 minutes.
3. Heat an outdoor grill for medium-high heat and lightly oil the grate.
4. Remove meat from marinade and slide it onto the skewers.
5. Lay the skewers on the grill and cook, turning every three minutes until meat is no longer pink and juices run clear.
6. Serve hot on rolls.

Grilled Virginia Ham and Cheese Sandwich

Virginia ham, a type of country ham, is salt-cured for three months and then usually smoked. The meat is traditionally stored in a burlap bag and aged for at least four more months. Ham prepared in this way will last at room temperature for several years.

Baking a Virginia ham is a lot of work. The first step is to scrub the ham with a stiff brush to scrape off any mold. Believe it or not, it is fine to eat the ham once the mold is gone. The ham then needs to be submerged in water for up to three days, with the water being replaced often, and the ham scrubbed again. Finally, the ham is placed in a roasting bag with water and a little flour and baked in the oven.

Virginia ham is a popular food in Virginia and is often served at holiday meals. The meat is thick, fatty, and salty, and can be prepared in many different ways. People in some areas, especially in St. Mary's County, Maryland, stuff Virginia hams with kale, collard greens, and cayenne pepper, then boil them for several hours. The result is a strong-flavored delicacy. Instead of stuffing the ham, other people like to coat it with orange juice and brown sugar while it finishes baking in the oven. No matter how it's cooked, leftovers can be used to make sandwiches, soups, or stews. This recipe uses Virginia ham in a hot sandwich.

Preparation Time: 5 minutes
Cooking Time: 5 minutes
Serves: 2

Ingredients

4 slices bread
4 slices Virginia ham
4 slices American or
    cheddar cheese
Shredded lettuce (optional)
Butter

1. Top each of 2 slices of bread with 1 slice of cheese, a handful of shredded lettuce (optional), 2 slices of ham, and then the last slice of cheese. Close each sandwich with another slice of bread.
2. Butter both sandwiches on the outside.
3. Place the sandwiches in a frying pan. Cook over medium heat until bread browns and cheese begins to melt.
4. Flip the sandwiches over and brown the other side.
5. Remove from pan, cut each sandwich in half, and serve.

Virginia ham is sometimes served with red-eye gravy, made from mixing strong coffee and sugar into the ham drippings. The fat forms "red eyes" of grease in the gravy, giving the dish its name.

Cranberry Sauce

New Jersey is one of the leading producers of cranberries in the United States. This tart but tasty fruit grows in a type of wetland called a bog. Cranberries can be eaten fresh or dried, or made into juice. Cranberry sauce is a popular side dish, especially at Thanksgiving dinner.

Preparation Time: 5 minutes
Cooking Time: 10 minutes
Makes: About 2 cups

Ingredients

2 cups cranberries
1 cup orange juice
½ cup sugar
1 orange, seeded, cut into slim pieces, with skin still on

1. Rinse cranberries thoroughly. Chop them with a blender or food processor.
2. In a saucepan, bring orange juice to a boil. Add cranberries and sugar. Cook for about 10 minutes.
3. Skim off any white froth on the surface.
4. Add orange pieces and stir to mix.
5. Pour sauce into a serving dish and let it cool.

Corn Pudding

Corn pudding is a Maryland favorite that is often served at church suppers and other community get-togethers. This recipe is a great example of how traditional Mid-Atlantic cooking takes a common vegetable and makes it something special.

Preparation Time: 10 minutes
Cooking Time: 45 minutes
Serves: 6 to 8

Ingredients

2 eggs
1 cup milk
pinch of sugar
pinch of salt
1 tablespoon cornstarch or flour
1 small onion, diced
1 8½-ounce can creamed corn
1 7-ounce can whole kernel corn
Butter

1. Preheat oven to 350°F.
2. In a bowl, mix eggs, milk, sugar, and salt.
3. Whisk in cornstarch or flour until smooth.
4. Add onion and both cans of corn. Mix thoroughly.
5. Butter a 7 x 7-inch casserole dish. Pour in corn mixture. Bake for 45 minutes or until puffy and golden on top.
6. Serve hot.

Baked Squash

Squash is a common ingredient in Mid-Atlantic cooking. It comes in many varieties, including pumpkins, butternut squash, Hubbard squash, acorn squash, summer squash, and zucchini. Early settlers loved this vitamin-packed vegetable, which could be served in many different ways and also stayed fresh throughout the winter. This baked squash dish uses an easy, traditional recipe. It can be served as a side dish with almost any main course.

Preparation Time: 5 minutes
Cooking Time: 1 hour
Serves: 4 to 6

Ingredients

2 acorn squash or one butternut squash,
    cut in half and seeds removed
4 tablespoons butter
Maple syrup or brown sugar

Optional Filling:
1 apple, peeled and diced
½ cup raisins

1. Preheat oven to 350°F.
2. Place squash cut side down in a baking dish. Pour in water halfway up the squash.
3. Bake for 35 to 40 minutes or until almost cooked.
4. Remove pan from oven and drain liquid from pan.
5. Turn squash upright and dot with butter.
6. Drizzle with maple syrup or brown sugar.
7. Stuff with apple raisin mixture, if desired.
8. Return pan to oven and bake for another 20 minutes.
9. Serve hot!

New York State
Apple Muffins

The apple is the official fruit of New York and is farmed all across the state. This recipe was created by elementary school students in North Syracuse, New York, and was voted the official muffin of New York State.

Preparation Time: 35 minutes
Cooking Time: 20 to 25 minutes
Makes: 2 dozen muffins

Ingredients

Topping:
½ cup walnuts
½ cup brown sugar
¼ cup flour
1 teaspoon cinnamon
2 tablespoons
    melted butter

Muffins:
2 cups flour
¾ cup brown sugar
½ cup sugar
½ teaspoon salt
1½ teaspoons cinnamon
⅛ teaspoon nutmeg
2 teaspoons baking soda
2 cups apples, coarsely chopped
½ cup raisins
½ cup walnuts
3 eggs, slightly beaten
½ cup butter, melted
4 ounces cream cheese, cut into small pieces
½ teaspoon vanilla

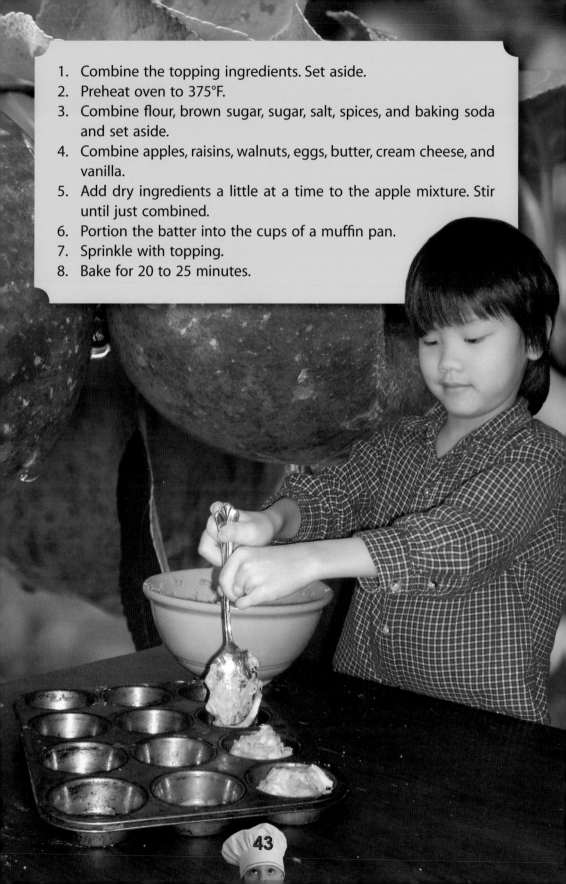

1. Combine the topping ingredients. Set aside.
2. Preheat oven to 375°F.
3. Combine flour, brown sugar, sugar, salt, spices, and baking soda and set aside.
4. Combine apples, raisins, walnuts, eggs, butter, cream cheese, and vanilla.
5. Add dry ingredients a little at a time to the apple mixture. Stir until just combined.
6. Portion the batter into the cups of a muffin pan.
7. Sprinkle with topping.
8. Bake for 20 to 25 minutes.

Hoecakes

In colonial times, this corn cake was baked on the back of a hoe, or shovel, that was greased with beef fat and placed over an open fire. Today it is much easier to make using a pan on the stove!

Preparation Time: 5 minutes
Cooking Time: 20 minutes
Serves: 6 to 10 (makes 2 cakes)

Ingredients

2 cups yellow cornmeal
1 teaspoon salt
Milk
Butter (optional)

1. Sift cornmeal and salt together. Stir in enough milk to make a soft dough. The mixture should not be runny!
2. Pour dough into a well-greased skillet, about ½ inch deep.
3. Cook slowly for 15 minutes until brown. Using a spatula, flip it over and brown the other side. Test for doneness by inserting a toothpick in the center and pulling it out. If the toothpick comes out clean, the hoecake is done.
4. Cook the rest of the batter the same way.
5. Cut into slices and serve hot. Top with butter if you want.

Beaten Biscuits

These fluffy biscuits from Maryland were originally "beaten" with a hammer or a mallet, but now a food processor or mixer can be used to beat the dough. Beaten biscuits taste great with scrambled eggs for breakfast, with gravy for dinner, or topped with juicy sliced berries for dessert.

Preparation Time: 15 minutes
Cooking Time: 20 minutes
Serves: 6

Ingredients

1 cup flour
¼ cup vegetable shortening
¼ teaspoon salt
¼ teaspoon baking soda
¼ teaspoon sugar
½ to ¾ cup water
Butter or jam (optional)

1. Preheat oven to 400°F.
2. Pour all ingredients except water into a food processor or mixer and blend.
3. Slowly add enough water to make the dough soft.
4. Remove dough from processor and place on a floured surface.
5. Divide dough into 6 parts and roll each part into a ball. Knead until smooth.
6. Place each ball of dough on a lightly buttered baking dish and flatten slightly with a fork. Prick the top of each biscuit 2–3 times with the fork.
7. Bake 20 minutes or until golden. If the bottoms start to get too dark, turn the biscuits over and finish cooking them.

8. Serve warm, and top with butter and jam if you want.

Black and White Cookies

This cookie is sometimes called a half moon or a half and half. It is very popular in New York and is sometimes marketed as the New York Black and White Cookie. Different parts of the state bake different styles of cookies, with some bakers using puffy cookies and others using a drier cookie base. Some recipes call for a hint of lemon in the cookie, some call for lemon in the icing, and others leave out the lemon altogether. Either way, these are a delicious treat!

Preparation Time: 15 minutes
Cooking Time: 15 to 17 minutes
Makes: 12 to 16 cookies

Ingredients

For cookies:
2 1/2 cups all-purpose flour
1 teaspoon baking soda
1 teaspoon salt
2/3 cup buttermilk
1 teaspoon vanilla
2/3 cup (10 2/3 tablespoons) butter, softened
1 cup granulated sugar
2 large eggs

For icing:
3 cups confectioners' sugar
2 tablespoons light corn syrup
4 teaspoons lemon juice
1/2 teaspoon vanilla
4 tablespoons water
1/2 cup unsweetened cocoa powder

Cookies:
1. Preheat oven to 350°F.
2. Whisk together flour, baking soda, and salt in a bowl. Stir together buttermilk and vanilla in a cup.
3. Beat together butter and sugar in a large bowl with an electric mixer until pale and fluffy, about 3 minutes.
4. Add egg, beating until well combined.
5. Mix in flour mixture and buttermilk mixture alternately in batches with a mixer at low speed, scraping down the side of the bowl occasionally. Mix until smooth.
6. Spoon ¼ cup of batter about 2 inches apart onto a buttered large baking sheet. Bake in middle of oven until tops are puffed and pale golden, and cookies spring back when touched, about 15 to 17 minutes.
7. Transfer with a metal spatula to a rack and cool. To chill them faster, put them in the refrigerator for about 5 minutes.

Icing:
1. Put confectioners' sugar, corn syrup, lemon juice, vanilla, and 1 tablespoon water in a small bowl. Stir until smooth.
2. Transfer half of icing to another bowl and stir in cocoa, adding more water, ½ teaspoon at a time, to thin it out to the same consistency as the white icing.
3. Turn cookies flat side up. Spread white icing over half of each cookie and chocolate icing over the other half. To make a crisp line between the two colors, place the flat edge of a table knife or spatula across the middle of the cookie as you ice it.

Apple Dumplings

These filling and delicious treats are an Amish specialty. They are usually sold individually at country markets and bakeries in Pennsylvania and are best eaten hot. My husband makes them, but the best one I ever had was at the Apple Festival at Peddler's Village in Lahaska, Pennsylvania.

Preparation Time: 20 minutes
Cooking Time: 40 minutes
Serves: 6

Ingredients

2 cups all-purpose flour
$2^{1/2}$ teaspoons baking powder
$1/2$ teaspoon salt
2 sticks butter or margarine
$1/2$ cup milk
6 baking apples (Granny Smith apples work well), washed, peeled, and cored
2 cups lightly packed light brown sugar
2 cups water
$1/8$ teaspoon ground cinnamon
$1/8$ teaspoon ground nutmeg
Whipped cream or vanilla ice cream (optional)

1. Preheat oven to 375°F.
2. Sift flour, baking powder, and salt together.
3. Add $2/3$ cup of butter to the flour mixture until soft and crumbly.
4. Sprinkle milk over the mixture until moist, pressing it into a ball.
5. Roll out the dough to about $1/4$ inch thick on a floured surface, and cut into 6-inch squares.
6. Place an apple on each square and bring the dough up and around the apple to cover it completely.
7. Moisten the top edges with water to make them stick together.

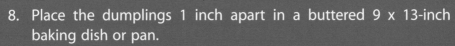

8. Place the dumplings 1 inch apart in a buttered 9 x 13-inch baking dish or pan.
9. Combine the brown sugar, water, cinnamon, and nutmeg in a large saucepan and bring to a boil. Simmer over low heat for 3 minutes. Remove from heat and stir in the remaining butter.
10. Pour syrup over dumplings.
11. Bake for 35 to 40 minutes, basting every 10 to 15 minutes.
12. Serve hot with whipped cream or vanilla ice cream on top.

Delaware
Peach Cobbler

The peach blossom is Delaware's state flower, and in the 1800s, southern Delaware was the main producer of peaches in the country. Peaches are still a popular fruit in the state, and this recipe uses them to make a refreshing dessert.

Preparation Time: 20 minutes
Cooking Time: 50 to 55 minutes
Serves: 8

Ingredients

4 cups fresh or thawed frozen
    peaches, peeled and sliced
1½ cups sugar, divided
½ teaspoon almond extract
½ cup butter or margarine,
    melted
¾ cup all-purpose flour
2 teaspoons baking soda
Pinch of salt
¾ cup milk
Ice cream (optional)

1. In a large bowl, toss peaches, 1 cup of sugar, and extract; set aside.
2. Pour butter into a 2-quart baking dish.
3. In another bowl, combine flour, baking powder, salt, and the rest of the sugar; stir in milk.
4. Pour the milk mixture evenly over butter (do not stir). Top with peach mixture.
5. Bake at 350°F for 50 to 55 minutes or until golden brown.
6. Serve with ice cream, if desired.

Sweet Potato Pudding

The sweet potato—or yam—has grown in southern Africa for over 5,000 years. Settlers discovered that like the squash, this was another hearty, healthy vegetable that was easy to store and could be used in a variety of dishes. This dessert recipe is African American in origin. It is similar to bread pudding and makes a sweet dessert.

Preparation Time: 20 minutes
Cooking Time: 45 to 60 minutes
Serves: 6

Ingredients

3 medium sweet potatoes
3 eggs, beaten
½ stick margarine or butter, melted
½ cup granulated sugar
½ cup all-purpose flour
1 tablespoon vanilla
¼ teaspoon ground cinnamon
¼ teaspoon ground nutmeg
½ cup raisins
½ cup milk

1. Boil the sweet potatoes. When they are tender, drop them in cold water and slip off the skins.
2. Preheat oven to 350°F.
3. Butter a 7½-inch round baking dish.
4. In a bowl, mash the potatoes with a spoon or mixer. Set aside.
5. In another bowl, mix the rest of the ingredients, then mix them with the mashed potatoes. Pour it all into the baking dish.
6. Bake approximately 45 to 60 minutes or until the top is lightly browned.

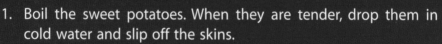

Fasnachts

Also known as potato doughnuts, fasnachts are always baked for Shrove Tuesday (the day before Ash Wednesday). Known as Mardi Gras or Fat Tuesday in some parts of the world, Shrove Tuesday is the last day before the start of Lent in the Catholic religion. Because sugar, fat, and eggs are prohibited during Lent, people used to use up these ingredients to make pancakes as a "last feast." Thus, Shrove Tuesday is sometimes called Pancake Day. In Germany, the tradition is to make doughnuts instead of pancakes. The Amish people continue this tradition with these potato doughnuts.

Preparation Time: 30 minutes
Cooking Time: 10 minutes
Makes: About 26

Ingredients

1 cup milk
1 cup cooked mashed potatoes
⅔ cup granulated sugar
½ teaspoon salt
3 tablespoons butter
3 tablespoons margarine
2 large eggs, lightly beaten
1 package active dry yeast
¼ cup lukewarm water
6 cups all-purpose flour
Vegetable oil for frying
Granulated sugar for coating

1. Scald the milk and let it cool to lukewarm.
2. While milk is cooling, blend the mashed potatoes, sugar, salt, butter, and margarine in a large bowl.
3. Gradually add beaten eggs and stir until creamy.

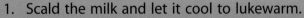

4. Dissolve the yeast in lukewarm water and add to potato mixture.
5. Alternate adding milk and flour, mixing until the dough is smooth and stretchy.
6. Turn the dough into a large buttered bowl, turning until all sides are buttered.
7. Cover and set in a warm, draft-free area. Let the dough rise until doubled, about 45 minutes.
8. Punch or knead the dough to remove all the bubbles.
9. Divide the dough in half and roll out to about ¾-inch thick.
10. Cut into 3-inch squares, and make a 1-inch diagonal slit in each square with a buttered knife.
11. Cover squares and let rise until they double in size.
12. Heat 3 inches of oil in a pan until very hot. Drop in each square and fry until golden brown on both sides.
13. Drain on paper towels.
14. Shake on sugar while fasnachts are still warm.

Honey Cookies

These traditional cookies were brought to Baltimore, Maryland, by Polish immigrants. They can be used as Christmas tree decorations by sprinkling them with colored sugars. They are quick to bake, and their Polish name, *Piernik Gwaltu! Goscie Jada*, means "Hurry, guests are coming!"

Preparation Time: 15 minutes
Cooking Time: 12 minutes per tray
Makes: About 24 cookies

Ingredients

2 eggs
1 cup granulated sugar
1 cup honey
1 teaspoon vanilla
2 teaspoons baking soda
1 tablespoon water
4½ cups all-purpose flour
2 teaspoons baking powder
1 teaspoon salt
1 egg, beaten, for glaze
Sugar

1. Preheat oven to 350°F.
2. In a large bowl, beat eggs until they are light and fluffy.
3. Add sugar, honey, and vanilla. Whisk until blended.
4. In a small bowl, dissolve the baking soda in water and add to the egg and honey mixture.
5. Sift flour, baking powder, and salt together. Gradually add to the egg and honey mixture until a soft dough forms.
6. Divide dough in half. On a floured surface, roll half the dough out to ⅛ inch thick. Cut into shapes with cookie cutters.

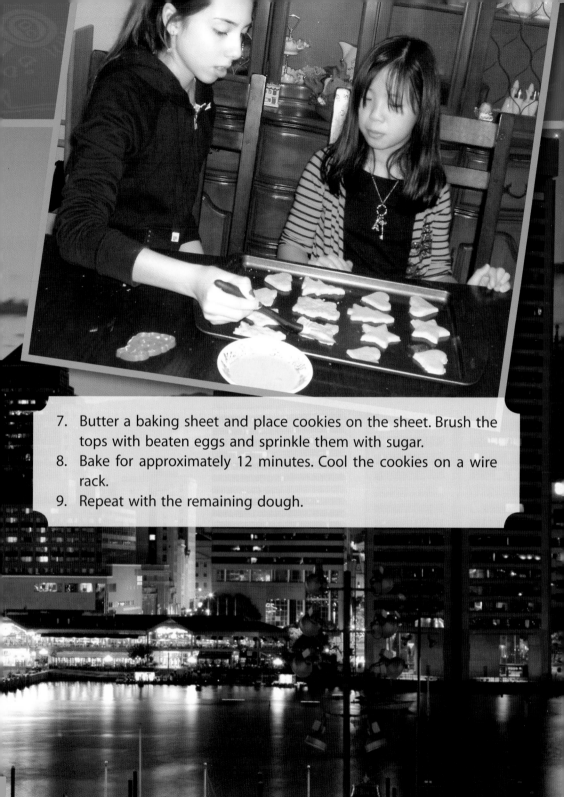

7. Butter a baking sheet and place cookies on the sheet. Brush the tops with beaten eggs and sprinkle them with sugar.
8. Bake for approximately 12 minutes. Cool the cookies on a wire rack.
9. Repeat with the remaining dough.

Books

Cook, Deanna. *The Kids' Multicultural Cookbook.* Charlotte, Vermont: Williamson Books, 2008.

D'Amico, Joan, and Karen E. Drummond. *The U.S. History Cookbook: Delicious Recipes and Exciting Events from the Past.* Hoboken, New Jersey: John Wiley and Sons, 2003.

Libal, Joyce. *Mid-Atlantic. American Regional Cooking Library.* Broomall, Pennsylvania: Mason Crest Publishers, 2005.

Webb, Lois Sinaiko. *The Multicultural Cookbook for Students.* Westport, Connecticut: Greenwood, 2009.

On the Internet

Eat Like a President: 50+ White House Recipes You Can Enjoy
http://www.nowpublic.com/style/eat-president-50-white-house-recipes-you-can-enjoy

Food History
http://www.kitchenproject.com

Food Timeline
http://www.foodtimeline.org/foodfaq4.html

The History of Potato Chips
http://www.kitchenproject.com/history/AmericanHeritageRecipes/PotatoChip.htm

Kids Cooking in the USA: Recipes from All 50 States
http://homeschooling.about.com/od/kidscookingintheusa/

State History
http://www.theus50.com

State of New Jersey Department of Agriculture: Jersey Fresh
http://www.jerseyfresh.nj.gov/

Works Consulted

Allrecipes.com
http://www.allrecipes.com

Anchor Bar: "The Original Since 1964"
http://www.anchorbar.com/original.php

Bower, Anne. *African American Foodways: Exploration and History of Cultures.* Urbana and Chicago: University of Illinois Press, 2007.

Cook, Anne Quinn. *Seasons of Pennsylvania: A Cookbook.* State College: Pennsylvania University Press, 2002.

The Cook's Thesaurus: Ham
http://www.foodsubs.com/MeatcureHams.html

"Delaware Peach Cobbler"
http://www.fiferorchards.com/recipes/peaches_016.php

Epicurious.com
http://www.epicurious.com

Fullinwider, Rowena J. *Celebrate Virginia Cookbook: The Hospitality, History, and Heritage of Virginia.* Nashville: Cool Springs Press, 2002.

Groff, Betty. *Betty Groff's Pennsylvania Dutch Cookbook.* New York: Galahad Books, 1990.

Hayes, Joanne Lamb. *Grandma's Wartime Kitchen: World War II and the Way We Cooked.* New York: St. Martin's Press, 2000.

McKee, Gwen, and Barbara Moseley, eds. *Best of the Best from the Mid-Atlantic Cookbook: Selected Recipes from the Favorite Cookbooks of Maryland, Delaware, New Jersey, and Washington, D.C.* Brandon, Missouri: Quail Ridge Press, 2001.

"Making a Virginia Ham"
http://www.slashfood.com/2008/12/09/making-a-virginia-ham/

Pat's King of Steaks: "About Us"
http://www.patskingofsteaks.com/aboutus.html

"Saratoga Chips: A Saratoga Springs NY Invention Resulting in Today's Potato Chips" http://www.saratoga.com/news/saratoga-chips.cfm

Smith, Irina, and Ann Hazan. *The Original Baltimore Neighborhood Cookbook.* Philadelphia: Camino Books, 1991.

"St. Mary's County Spicy Stuffed Ham"
http://recipes.epicurean.com/recipe/1335/st.-marys-county-spicy-stuffed-ham.htm

Stradley, Linda. "History of Manhattan Clam Chowder." *What's Cooking America,* 2004.
http://whatscookingamerica.net/History/Chowder/ManhattanChowder.htm

Varozza, Georgia. *The Homestyle Amish Kitchen Cookbook.* Eugene, Oregon: Harvest House Publishers, 2010.

"White House Presidential Recipes Through the Years"
http://blogpublic.lib.msu.edu/index.php/2006/02/20/white_house_presidential_recipes_through?blog=5

baste (BAYST)—To drizzle or brush liquid over food while it is cooking.

beat (BEET)—To mix quickly with a fork or electric mixer.

brittle (BRIH-tul)—Candy made with sugar and nuts and spread in thin sheets.

broil (BROYL)—To cook directly under a source of high heat.

broiler pan (BROY-lur PAN)—A deep-sided nonstick pan that has a grate on which to place the food as it cooks; the bottom pan can hold liquids to season the food, and it catches drips as the food cooks.

cartilage (KAR-tuh-lidj)—Stretchy tissue that is part of an animal's skeleton.

casserole dish (KASS-uh-rohl DISH)—A baking dish with high sides that can be placed in the oven.

chowder (CHOW-dur)—A soup made with broth or cream, vegetables, potatoes, and meat or fish.

colander (KAH-lun-dur)—A metal or heavy plastic bowl with holes, used to drain water from food.

core (KOR)—To cut the seeds and tough center out of an apple or other fruit.

dice (DYS)—To cut into small cubes.

drizzle (DRIH-zul)—To pour in small amounts, gently.

dumpling (DUMP-ling)—A small ball of dough that is cooked by steaming or boiling in liquid such as broth or gravy.

ethnic (ETH-nik)—Having to do with the culture and customs of a group of people.

grease (GREES)—To spread shortening, oil, or butter on a pan or cookie sheet to prevent food from sticking to it.

immigrant (IH-muh-grunt)—A person who comes from somewhere else to settle in a new country.

knead (NEED)—To work dough with your hands to make it smooth.

marinate (MAH-ruh-nayt)—To soak meat or other food in a sauce before cooking.

Old Bay® seasoning (OLD BAY SEE-zuh-ning)—A mix of spices commonly used in Mid-Atlantic cooking, especially on seafood and french fries.

saucepan (SOS-pan)—A small cooking pot with a handle.

shish kebab (SHISH kuh-BOB)—Meat and vegetables placed on a skewer and cooked on a grill.

shortening (SHORT-ning)—A type of thick vegetable oil used in cooking.

sift (SIFT)—To put a dry substance, such as flour, through a sieve to break up any lumps.

simmer (SIH-mur)—To cook gently for a long time over low heat, keeping to just under a boil.

skewer (SKYOO-ur)—A long wooden or metal rod on which food is threaded for cooking.

skillet (SKIH-lit)—A shallow pan used to fry food.

utensil (yoo-TEN-sil)—Any of the tools used in the kitchen, such as a spoon or fork.

vendor (VEN-dor)—A person who sells things.

venison (VEH-nih-sun)—Meat from a deer.

whisk (WISK)—To mix quickly with a wire kitchen utensil (called a whisk).

Worcestershire sauce (WUSS-tur-shir SAWSS)—A strong-flavored sauce that includes garlic, soy sauce, and vinegar.

Index

About the
AUTHOR

Joanne Mattern has lived in New York State all her life. She was born near the banks of the Hudson River and grew up enjoying regional favorites and dishes from her Italian immigrant grandmother. Later, Joanne ventured into central New York State and discovered some of the delicious favorites from that area. She has also traveled extensively throughout the Mid-Atlantic region, from northern New York all the way down to Maryland and Washington, D.C., and has sampled and enjoyed many foods along the way. Today, Joanne continues to live in New York's Hudson Valley, where she enjoys cooking and trying new foods along with her husband (who is a chef and children's cooking instructor) and their four children.